DENNIS and THE FANTASTIC FOREST

by ADRIAN RAESIDE

Doubleday Canada Limited

To Mari

Canadian Cataloguing in Publication Data

Raeside, Adrian, 1957–
Dennis and the fantastic forest

ISBN 0-385-25531-4

I. Title

PS8585.A298D454 1997   jC813'.54   C96-932412-X
PZ7.R33De 1997

Cover art by Adrian Raeside
Text design by Heidy Lawrance Associates
Printed in Hong Kong

Published in Canada by
Doubleday Canada Limited
105 Bond Street
Toronto, Ontario M5B 1Y3

Dennis the Dragon was filling his pack
with picnic food for a hike up the track.
Chicken on doughnuts, green jelly in pastry,
Strawberry noodles—this *will* be tasty!

He put on his backpack, buckled it down
and set off for his favourite spot out of town.
When he got to the woods he sat down with a bump,
his beautiful trees were ugly black stumps.

Somebody must have been playing with fire—
and we all know that's what most dragons desire.
"My trees are all gone, burned up by a flame!
My fire-breathing brothers are surely to blame."

All of those trees—were they totally gone?
No! One tiny brown seed lay sadly alone.
Dennis worked busily back in his home
to give the small seed a place of its own.

He watered and chatted and took it for tea,
and in no time at all grew a little green tree.
Dennis said, "Now I'll return to the hill
with seedling and spade"—this gave him a thrill.

But one single tree looks lonely and thin.
"I'll replant the forest!" Dennis said with a grin.
Dennis turned into a planting machine,
before anyone knew it the hillside was green.

Dennis the Dragon could never stop there.
Hey, why not plant trees on ALL that is bare?
He planted the valleys, he planted the playgrounds,
he planted the rooftops, the fences, the duckponds.

In the blink of an eye the Dragonville scene
all disappeared in a tangle of green.
Trees crowded yards, trees waded streams,
trees sprouted from sofas and trees grew in jeans.

Dragonville people were shocked by these trees.
All of that greenery made some of them sneeze.
People ate trees as snacks, wore them as hats,
used them as shorts and dressed up their cats.

"Dennis," they cried, "this isn't too cool!
What good are these trees? We think you're a fool!"
Dennis was shocked to hear this protest.
Didn't they know that trees were the best?

"They're shade from the sun and they're good for the air.
They can make a canoe, a house or a chair.
We can swing on their branches or climb to the top.
If there's water below, what a splash when we drop!"

"And the very best thing about big leafy trees—
they're home to all kinds of bugs, birds and bees—
Squirrels and owls, green-tailed raccoons,
bluejays, chipmunks and red jackaroons."

But a few of those trees were still looking lean.
Remember those seedlings in sofas and jeans?
Dennis dug them all up and took them away
to plant in the forest the next sunny day.

It won't be so easy to burn those trees down
Now their protector can keep them around.
Who guards the forest from smouldering danger?
Dennis the Dragon, Official Park Ranger!

Those brothers who once nearly burned up the place?
They now have to face a foamy disgrace.